It's a sunny summer's day in Sunny Bay,
with the Sunny Town creatures
out to play.

For the crews of
the Royal National Lifeboat Institute,
heroes in human form
— P. A.

For the Lockdown babies:
Albert Gabrielle, George Davis,
George Ruffles, Isla Hughes,
Iris Goldsworthy-Trapp,
Maila Causton, Milo Mantle,
Otto Hamilton-Dyas,
Stevie Cullen
— B. M.

First published 2022 by Walker Books Ltd * 87 Vauxhall Walk, London SE11 5HJ * Text © 2022 Philip Ardagh * Illustrations © 2022 Ben Mantle
The right of Philip Ardagh and Ben Mantle to be identified as the author and illustrator respectively of this work has been asserted by them in
accordance with the Copyright, Designs and Patents Act 1988 * This book has been typeset in Archer Book * Printed in China * All rights reserved.
No part of this book may be reproduced, transmitted or stored in an information retrieval system in any form or by any means, graphic, electronic or
mechanical, including photocopying, taping and recording, without prior written permission from the publisher * British Library Cataloguing in
Publication Data: a catalogue record for this book is available from the British Library * ISBN 978-1-4063-9504-4 * www.walker.co.uk * 10 9 8 7 6 5 4 3 2 1

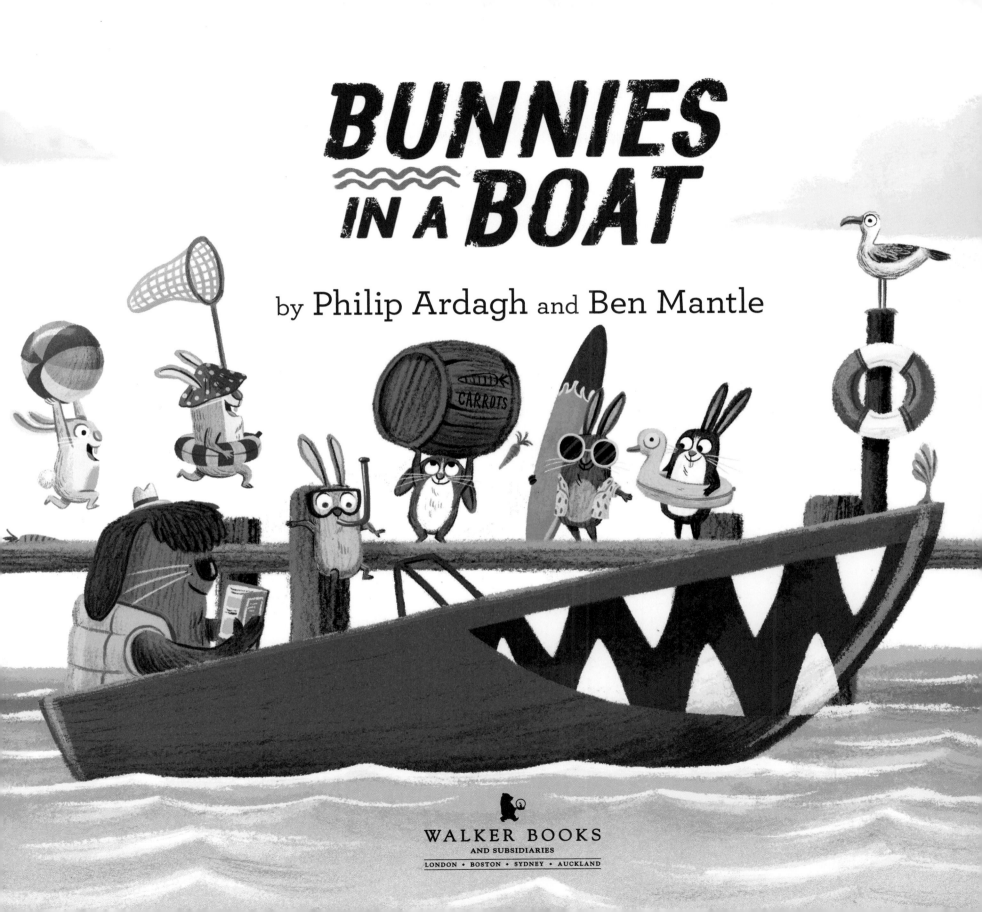

BUNNIES
IN A BOAT

by Philip Ardagh and Ben Mantle

WALKER BOOKS
AND SUBSIDIARIES
LONDON · BOSTON · SYDNEY · AUCKLAND

The penguins dive and paddle.
The turtles have a swim,
when WHOOSH goes a speed boat
and knocks poor Piggy in!

Bunnies in a boat!
Bunnies in a boat!

Dashing and a-splashing!
Let's hope they stay afloat!

Bunnies speeding past!
Bunnies speeding past!

Zipping through the water,
they're having such a BLAST!

Tigers on the sand!
Tigers on the sand!

Silly billy bunnies,
you can't take the boat on land!

Bunnies in a boat!
Bunnies in a boat!

Dashing and a-splashing!
Let's hope they stay afloat!

Hippos in the sea! Hippos in the sea!

VROOOOOOOOOOM!

Whoa!
That was a close one.
Oh deary, deary me!

The sheep are out there sailing.
It's such a lovely day.

Until the bunnies

vROOM right past them

and whisk their sails away!

Bunnies leaning over!
Bunnies jumping in the air!

Bunnies being naughty when they should be **TAKING CARE.**

There's a bunny in the water,
a bunny in the sea,
too busy eating carrots to cry out,
"Rescue me!"

Bunnies in a boat!

Bunnies in a boat!

Dashing and a-splashing!
Let's hope they stay afloat!

Bunnies at the jetty!
Bunnies at the jetty!

They've gone and hit the restaurant
and are COVERED IN SPAGHETTI!

Others come a-running
from all across the beach ...
but the bunnies are too fast for them
and are soon well out of reach.

Where are the bunnies heading for?
What can be their plan?
Why have they got that map out?
And where DID they get that van?

Oh NO!

Bunnies at the airport,
running for a plane,
heading for the cockpit...

SUNNY TOWN